The Magic Box

by Lazlo Barclay

Illustrations by Ellie Shakirova

Once upon a time,
in a rainforest far, far away

and in a treehouse high, high up,

there lived a young orangutan

named Ollie.

Ollie's favourite thing
in the whole wide world
was swinging and jumping
around the forest trees
with his three best friends...

Lisa,
the clever wild cat...

Tim,
the daring little squirrel...

...and Mo,
the big, friendly elephant!

Together, these four were the
funniest things in the whole rainforest.

They put on weird and wonderful shows
for all the other animals around, like this one –

"Predator or Prey – the Pantomime!"

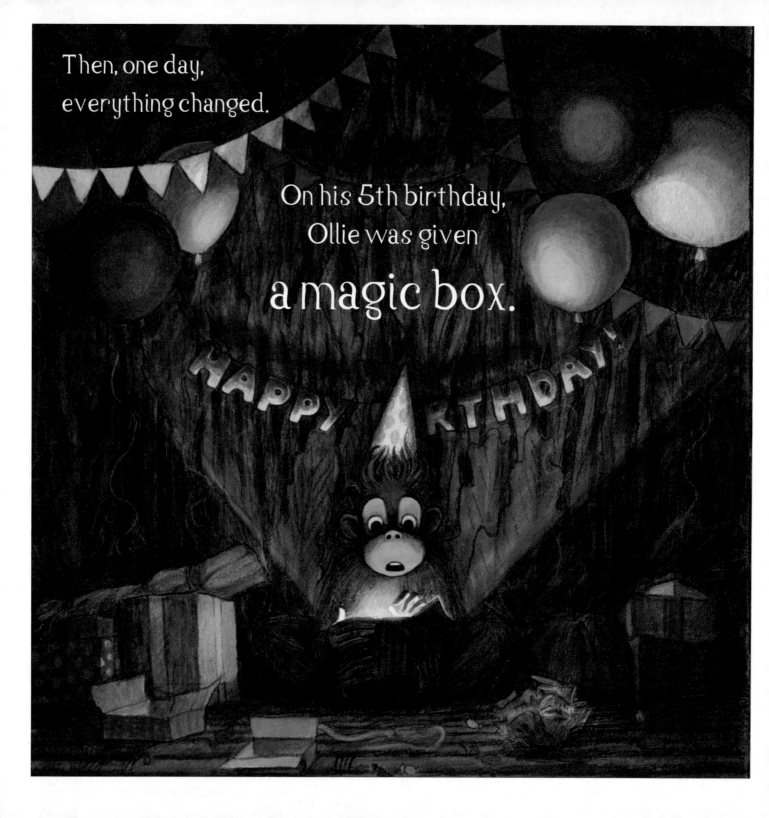

It was called a magic box because
inside it - just like magic - there was
a whole different world.

This different world
quickly became Ollie's favourite thing...

Though his friends still busily prepared for their next show, Ollie could do nothing but stare down at the magic box's bright screen.

He swiped, dragged, clicked and tapped...
swiped, dragged, clicked and tapped...
swiped, dragged, clicked and...

Eventually, after a few days,
Ollie no longer came out to play.
Instead, he stayed at home with his new toy.

Outside, in the real world,
his friends were left feeling sad.

"What shall we do?"

asked Mo, his ears drooping to the ground.
They had lost their best friend,
and the main character of their shows.

But Lisa wasn't going to give up that easily.
"I have a plan!"
she said.

That night, Tim snuck up into Ollie's treehouse and replaced his magic box with an old, broken one.

And Mo blew a letter all the loooong way up – to tell Ollie where he could fix it!

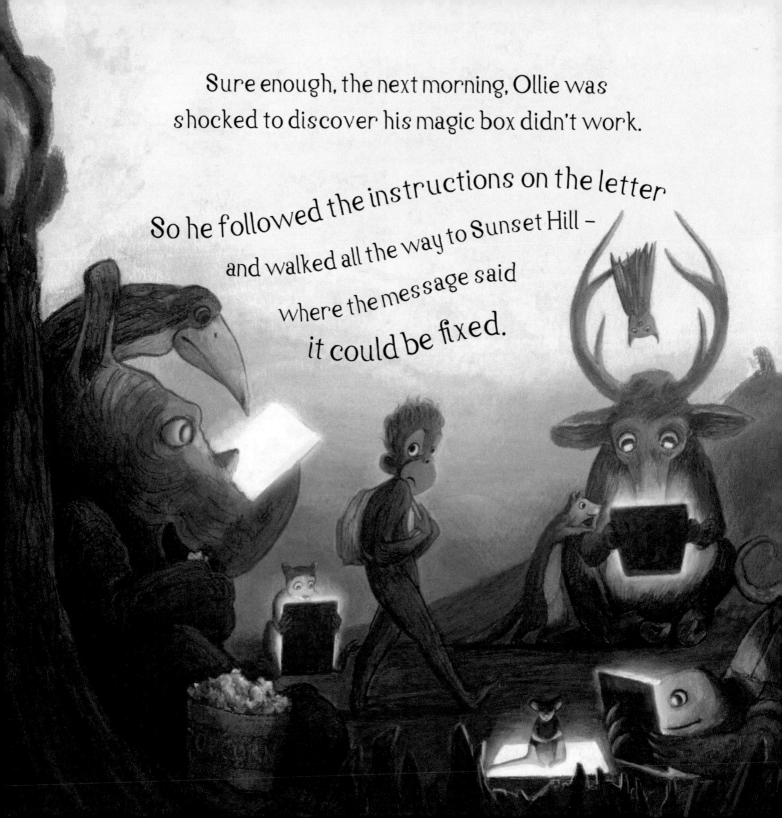

Sure enough, the next morning, Ollie was
shocked to discover his magic box didn't work.

So he followed the instructions on the letter
and walked all the way to Sunset Hill –
where the message said
it could be fixed.

What he found there was a very strange sight indeed.
Hundreds of animals, all on magic boxes!

He found Mo, Tim and Lisa on the top of the hill.

"Mo! Tim! Lisa! What's going on?"
asked Ollie.

The friends didn't move.

"Hey! Lisa? Mo? Tim? Can you hear me?"

The friends still didn't move.

"Why is everyone on magic boxes?!"
Ollie continued.
"Why won't anyone look up?!" he said.

Still nothing.

Ollie didn't understand.
He jumped on top of Mo,
and peered over
the elephant's head
to see what his friends
were all looking at.

There, written
across all three
magic boxes
in big shiny letters,
was the message:

Ollie thought for a while.

Hmmm...

What did they mean?

What had he looked like?

Maybe...

Those animals

"Mo! Tim! Lisa! I'm sorry for playing with my magic box and not with YOU!"

he shouted.

"I want to be friends with you again!"

Hurrah!
Ollie was back!

That morning, the friends went back
to their usual business.

They swung and jumped around the forest
even more cheekily, and got themselves
into all sorts of funny situations.

From that day on, Ollie kept the magic box
safely in his backpack, taking it out only when
he and his friends really needed it...

... Like taking selfies with all of their fans!

Lazlo Barclay, the author

Lazlo Barclay is a British-Peruvian writer and musician from London. He conceived the Magic Box as a way to raise future generations with a healthy attitude towards technology.

Ellie Shakirova, the illustrator

Ellie Shakirova is a Moscow-based artist who joined the project in spring 2018. She was instrumental in advising on the book's storyline in the early stages.